To

Charles

Love,

Granpa Joe + Yatlyn

2,009

This book belongs to

Charles Goldberg

Usborne Stories for little boys

Contents

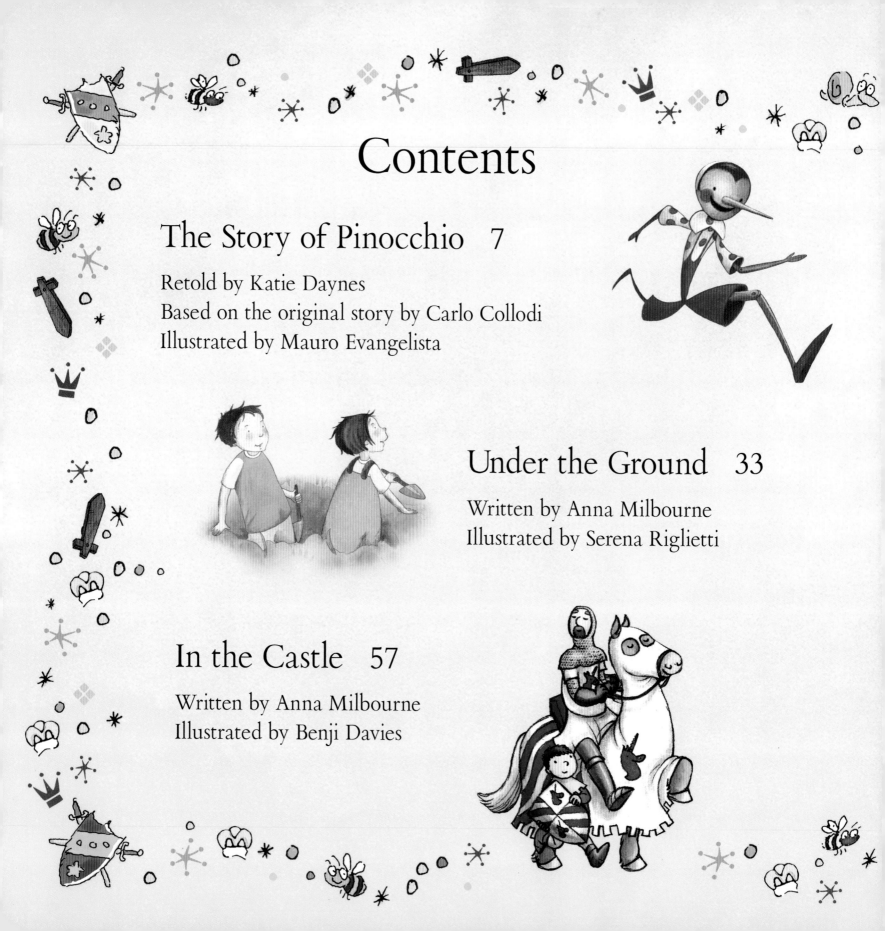

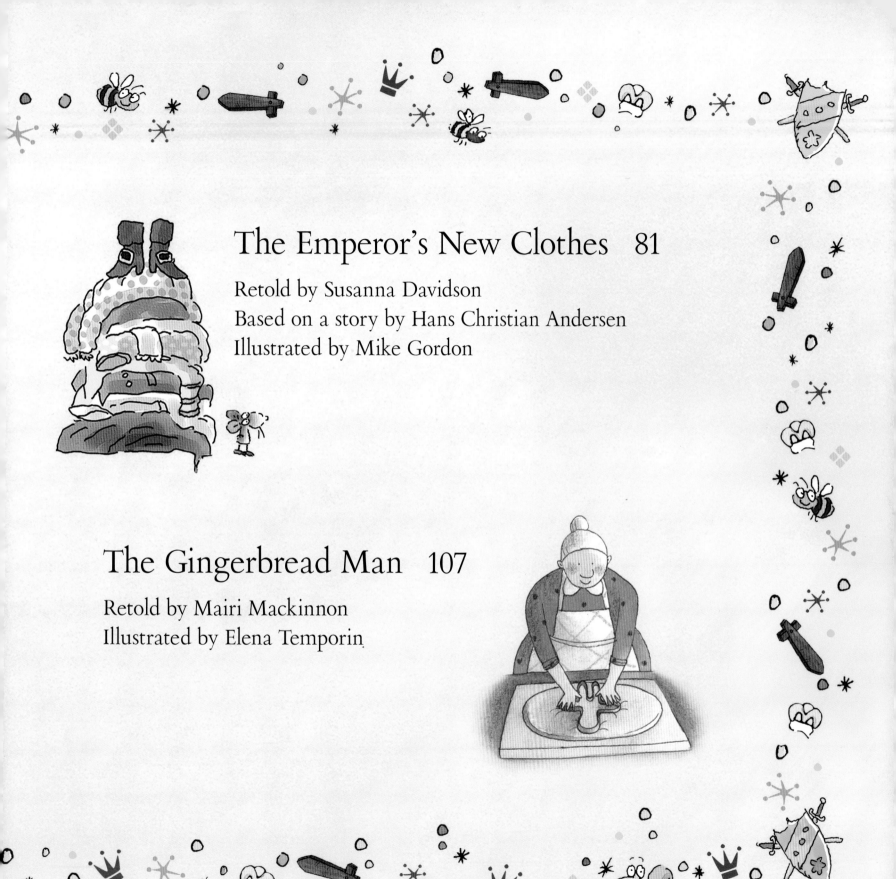

The Story of Pinocchio

Gepetto the carpenter had always wanted to make a puppet. One day, he found the perfect piece of wood.

He began by carving a head and a little nose.

Slowly, the nose grew...

longer...

and longer...

and longer.

Gepetto was astonished, but he kept on carving.

Hours later, he finished his long-nosed puppet and smiled.

Suddenly, the puppet jumped up, snatched Gepetto's wig and ran outside.

"Come back here, puppet!" Gepetto cried.

"I'm not a puppet," shouted the puppet. "My name is Pinocchio and I'm a *real* boy."

Pinocchio kept running, straight past a policeman.

"What's going on?" asked the policeman.
Then he saw Gepetto waving a chisel.
"Stop there, old man," he ordered. "You look dangerous."

"Tee hee," giggled
Pinocchio. He skipped
back home and snuggled
in an armchair by the fire.

buzzzzzzzzzzzzzz

"Foolish puppet,"
buzzed a cricket.

"Hey!" shouted Pinocchio. "I'm not a puppet. I'm a *real* boy."

"Oh no you're not," said the cricket. "You're a naughty puppet. Only good puppets become real boys."

Pinocchio was lost in thought...

until Gepetto arrived home with some supper.

"Er... Dad," said Pinocchio.
"I want to be a real boy."

Gepetto smiled.
"Well let's start by
sending you to school."

Be good,
Pinocchio!

15

On the way to school, Pinocchio saw a crowd of people.

"Are you here for the puppet show?" asked a well-dressed man.

"A puppet show?" said
Pinocchio. "Oh yes!"

He sold his school book,
bought a ticket...

...and dashed
into the show.

"Hello puppet," the performers called to Pinocchio. "Come and join us."

"We're going to the Land of Lost Toys," said a clown. "Do you want to come along?"

"I'd love to!" replied Pinocchio at once.

The Land of Lost Toys was one big funfair.

"Yippeeeeee!" squealed Pinocchio.

"Are you a lost toy too?"
asked a teddy bear.

"Um... yes," lied Pinocchio.
His wooden nose began to itch.

"I have no family," said the teddy bear.
"Nor do I," lied Pinocchio.

His itchy nose began to grow.

It grew

longer

and **longer**.

"Foolish puppet,"
buzzed a voice.
"You don't deserve
to be a real boy.
Your poor father is sick
with worry. He's rowing
across the ocean to find you."

"Oh no!" Pinocchio sighed. "I must
save him." Instantly, his nose began to shrink.

22

"I'll help you," cooed a pigeon.

Pinocchio jumped on her back
and they soared to the coast.

*Pinocchio?
Where are you?*

"There he is!"
cried Pinocchio.

As the puppet watched, a huge wave
rose up and swallowed Gepetto's boat.

"I'll save you, Dad!"
cried Pinocchio.

And he dived into the chilly water.

Pinocchio swam and swam... but there was no sign of Gepetto.

Then he felt a rush of water
and everything went dark.

"Where am I?" wondered Pinocchio, with a shudder.
Peering into the gloom, he saw a faint glow.

He followed it down a squelchy tunnel...

SQUELCH SQUELCH

...and stopped in surprise.

An old man was sitting at a desk.
"Dad?" whispered Pinocchio.

Pinocchio!

"I'm sorry I was so naughty," said Pinocchio.
"But don't worry, I'll get us out of here."

Pinocchio led Gepetto back along the dark, squelchy tunnel, to the mouth of a cave.

"Jump!" cried Pinocchio. "I'll tow you to the shore."

By midnight, Pinocchio and Gepetto were safely home.
"You're a good puppet," said Gepetto, kissing his son goodnight.

The next morning, Pinocchio woke
up feeling very different.

He was a real boy at last.

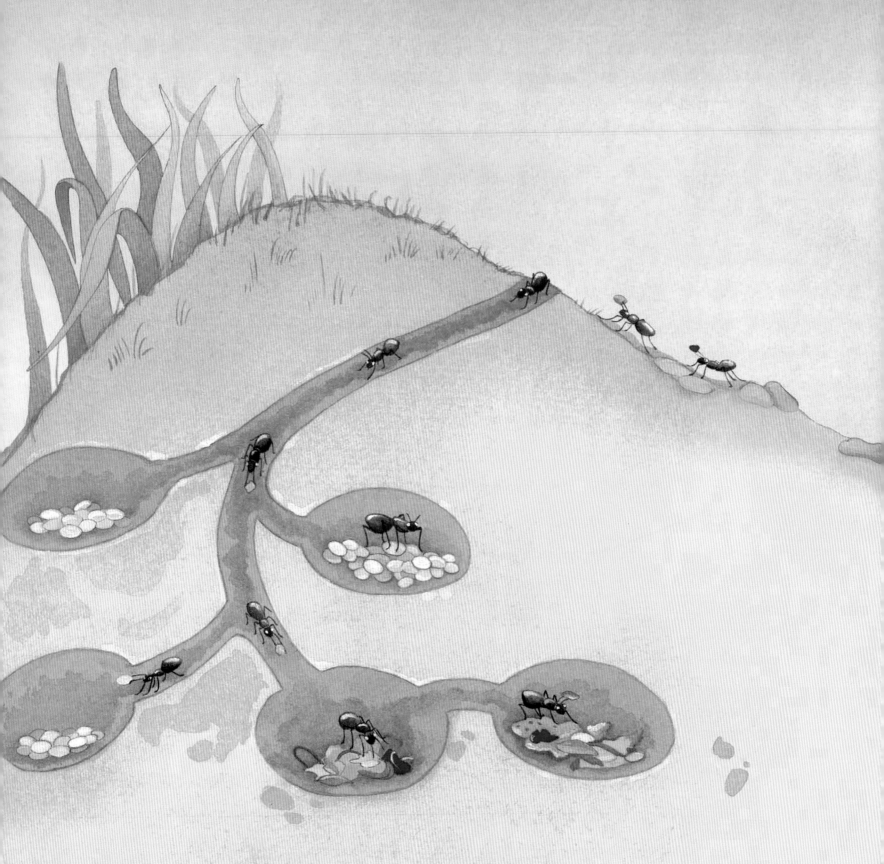

32

Under the Ground

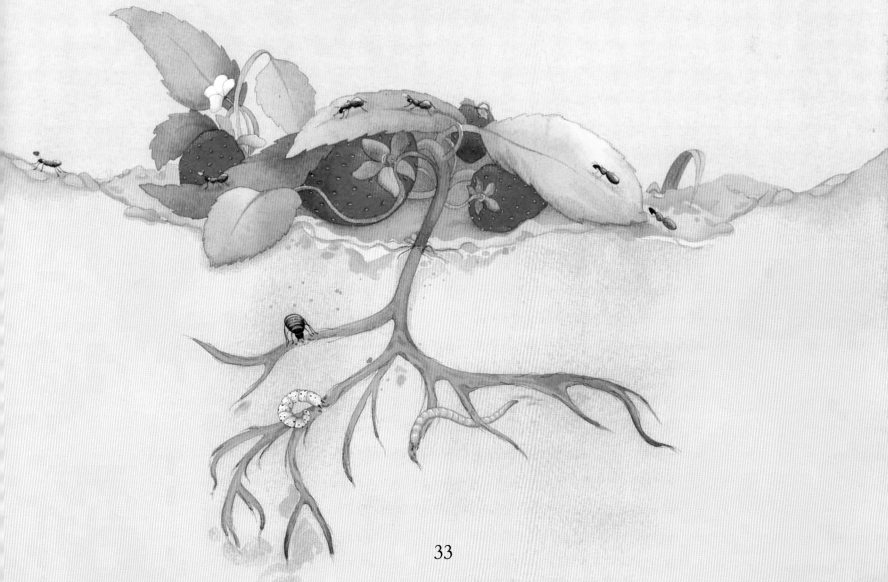

Have you ever wondered
what's under the ground?

There's a whole world down there
beneath your feet.

If you dug down a little way, you'd find...

...plant roots reaching out
to suck up water
from the soil...

...and hungry creepy-crawlies
munching through them.

Nearby, you might discover
a miniature kingdom...

...where a queen ant has laid
a thousand tiny eggs...

...and lots of little worker ants
are busy bringing food.

37

A little deeper, a snuffly mole
digs blindly through the soil.

He sniffs a juicy, wriggly worm,
tugs it out and slurps it down.

Running away from a fierce fox,
a rabbit leaps into her burrow...

...where her family is
cuddled up, safe and sound.

If you dug a little further, you'd see hundreds of criss-crossing pipes.

Some bring electricity to light up all the streetlamps...

...and some bring clean water to each and every house.

Other pipes carry dirty water away
from toilets, sinks and baths.

Robots crawl through them
to make sure none have sprung a leak.

There's a rumble in a tunnel and a train zoooOOOooms by.

Lots of trains rush around under the bustling streets of the city.

42

They carry people from
station to station, all day long.

Deeper still, there's solid rock,
patterned with stripes and swirls.

Buried in the rock...

...are the twirly shells of animals that lived long ago....

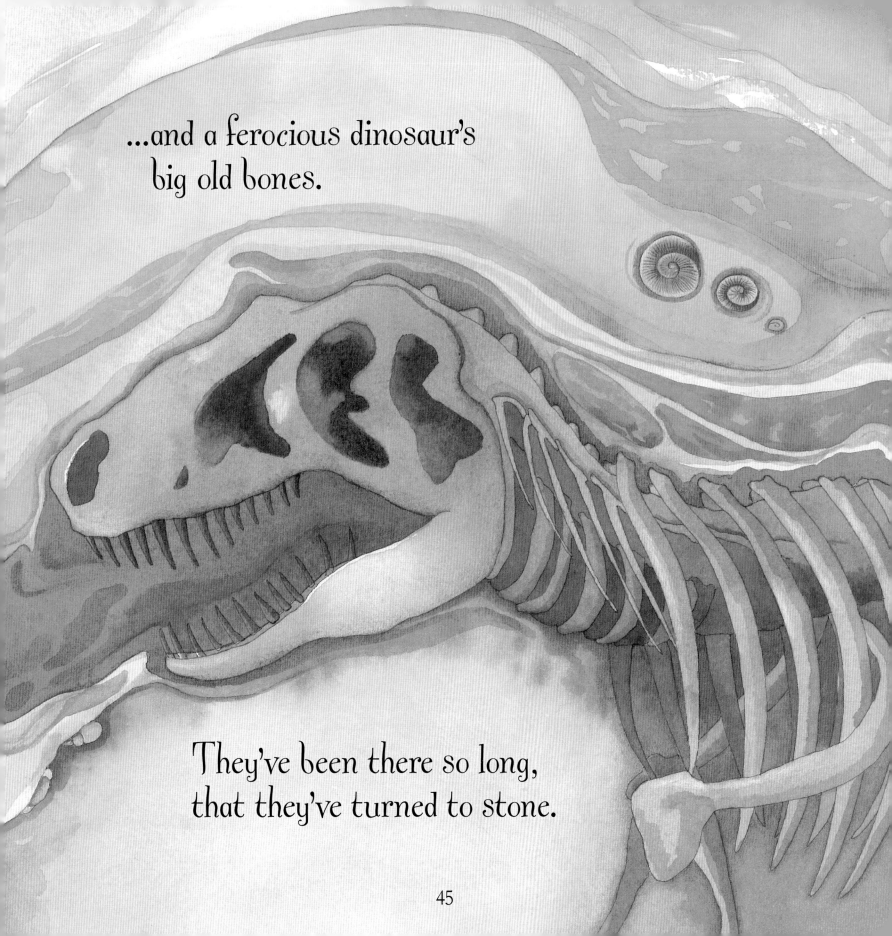

...and a ferocious dinosaur's
big old bones.

They've been there so long,
that they've turned to stone.

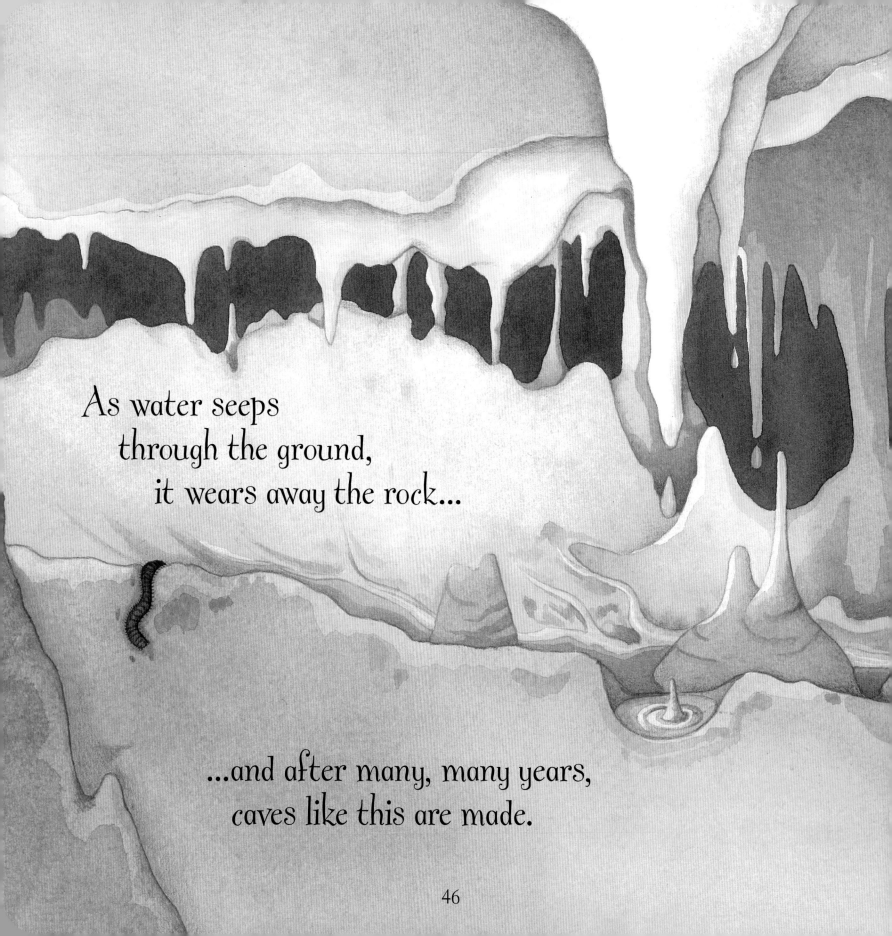

As water seeps
through the ground,
it wears away the rock...

...and after many, many years,
caves like this are made.

In some caves,
there are furry bats
dangling upside down.

Other caves are so deep and dark
that no one's EVER seen them.

Miles underground, twinkling silver and gold are hidden inside the rock.

Nobody put them there.
They're just part of the Earth.

People dig deep mines to find them.

They drill them
out of the rock...

...and take them away to make
into rings and other pretty things.

If you could dig even further underground,
you'd be deeper than anyone's ever been.

It gets hotter and hotter until
the rock melts into red gloop.

You'd melt too,
if you were really there.

The Earth is like an enormous ball.
This is it, chopped in half so you can see.

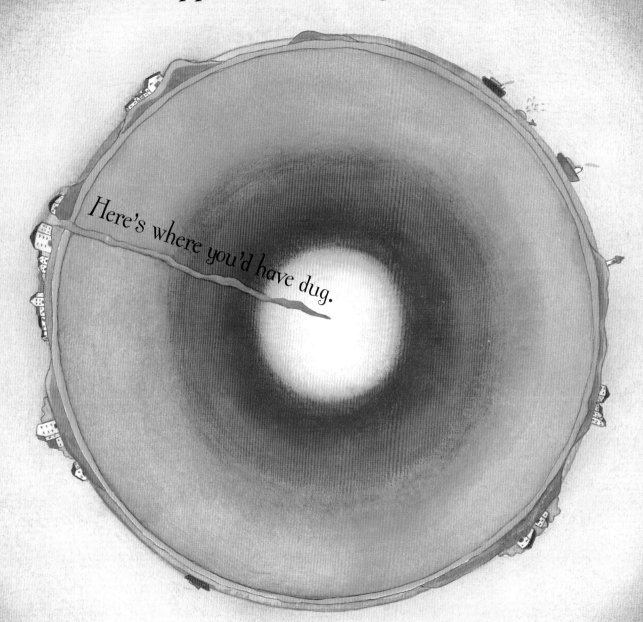

Here's where you'd have dug.

Right in the middle is the hottest part of all.

What do you think you'd find
if you kept on going?

You'd dig, dig, dig,
through stripy rock and bat-filled caves...

...past snuffly moles and tangled roots...

...and after that?

You'd pop out the other side of the world
on someone else's lawn...

...where they were busy wondering
what's under the ground.

In the Castle

Have you ever visited an old, tumbledown castle...

...and wondered what it was like to live there, long, long ago?

This castle belonged to a king and a queen.
But they didn't live in it alone.

Knights lived here too,
and ladies-in-waiting...

...and horses and blacksmiths and cooks.

It was a very
busy place indeed.

The king of the castle ordered everyone about.

He sent the knights
on exciting adventures.

And when they rushed back
with tales of all they'd done...

...the king's little nephew
would long to be a knight.

But first he'd have to learn to ride...

...and fight with
a wooden sword.

He'd help a real knight get ready...

...for each
heroic quest.

Later, when he was old enough...

...and brave enough...

66

...the king might make him a knight too.

He'd kneel before the throne.

"Arise Sir Knight!" the king would say,
and tap his shoulders with a sword.

From then on, his job would be to help keep the kingdom safe.

When enemies attacked, all the knights sprang into action.

They lifted up the drawbridge,
so no one could come in.

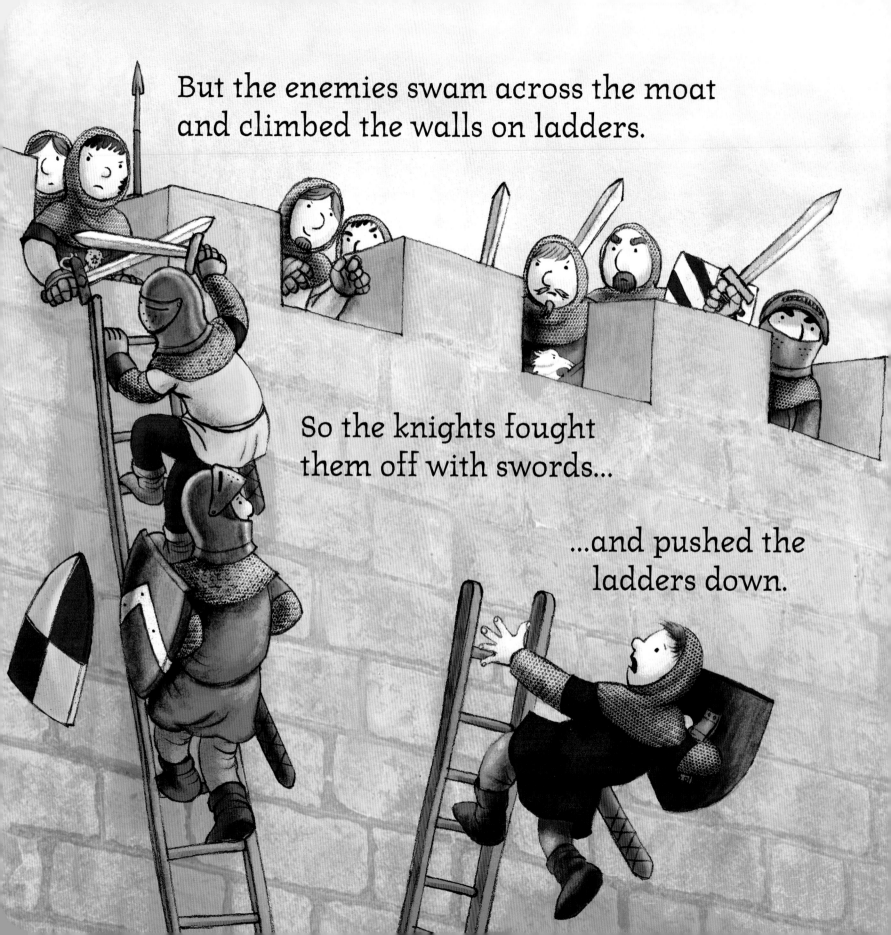

But the enemies swam across the moat and climbed the walls on ladders.

So the knights fought them off with swords...

...and pushed the ladders down.

Then they shot with bows and arrows...

...until the enemies
ran away.

To celebrate the victory,
the king and queen had a party.

They ate
roasted peacock
and fish with flowers...

...and honey cakes and gingerbread.

A jester clowned around and made everybody laugh.

The next day, they played jousting.

Two knights rode fast towards each other and tried to knock each other off.

It hurt quite a bit if you lost.

But if you won, you got a prize and everybody cheered.

Soon, the castle went back to normal.

The king gave orders
and ruled his kingdom.

The cooks cooked and the servants cleaned...

...and the knights did whatever they liked until they were needed again.

That was all a long, long time ago.

But just imagine if it weren't...

The Emperor's New Clothes

Once upon a time there was an
Emperor who loved clothes.

He liked looking splendid
ALL the time.

He had a different outfit for every day of the year.

But the Emperor had a problem. He had nothing to wear for the royal procession.

"Won't any of your outfits do, Your Highness?" asked his servant, Boris.

"NO!" said the Emperor.
"I want an outfit so splendid
that people will talk about me for years to come."

Boris sighed and set off to find the finest clothes-makers in town.

WANTED!
Splendid new outfit for the Emperor.
Clothes-makers apply here!

NO TIME-WASTERS PLEASE

He wasn't having much luck until...

a little round man

and a long thin man
rushed up to him.

They bowed with their
bottoms in the air.
"We are Slimus and
Slick, at your service,"
they said.

Boris took them to the Emperor.

"We make magic clothes," Slimus told him.
"Only clever people can see them. Stupid people can't!"

"Are they **splendid**?" asked the Emperor.
"Very **splendid**," promised Slick. "But very expensive.
We'll need pots and pots of money."

"Take all the money you want," cried the Emperor.
"Just make me those clothes!"

A week later, the Emperor and Boris went to see
Slimus and Slick at work. "Welcome!" they said.
"What do you think of our clothes?"

The Emperor gulped. Boris gulped.
Neither of them could see a thing.

But they didn't want to look stupid.
So the Emperor said, "Splendid!"
"Yes, really very... splendid," said Boris.

"Oh, um, er, most splendid!" added the footmen.

As soon as everyone had gone, Slimus and Slick laughed and laughed until their faces turned purple.

Then they ordered a huge feast.
"It's hungry work making magic clothes," they said.

On the morning of the
royal procession, the Emperor
couldn't wait to put on his new clothes.

"Here is your cloak," said Slimus.
"It's light as a feather."

"Oh Your Highness," said Slick. "You look
very handsome. Your clothes fit so well."

The Emperor admired himself
in the mirror. "Don't
I look *splendid?*"

"Yes, Your Highness," gasped the footmen, staring
straight at the Emperor.

"Yes, Your Highness," said Boris, staring straight at the ceiling. (He was trying NOT to look.)

"Open the palace gates!" ordered the Emperor. "Let the royal procession begin."

The crowd gasped
when they saw the Emperor.
Everyone had heard that only clever
people could see his clothes.

"Aren't his clothes **splendid**?" they said.

Extraordinary!

Fantastic!

Simply superb!

Splendiferous!

Wonderful!

Magnificent!

Amazing!

"Let me see him!"
called a small boy,
who was stuck
at the back of
the crowd.

"Ooh!" said the boy.
"The Emperor's got
no clothes on!"

Faster than a spreading fire,
a whisper whizzed
through the crowd.

The Emperor's got no clothes on!

The Emperor heard their words. He looked down.
"Oh no," he thought. "I'm naked!"

Then he blushed
bright red.

"But I can't stop now. This is the
royal procession and I am the Emperor."
So he held his head high and walked on.

The crowd clapped and cheered. They thought
it was the most splendid royal procession ever!

Meanwhile, Slimus and Slick were packing their bags full of money, getting ready to flee the palace forever.

A toast to invisible clothes!

"We tricked him!" they cried and cackled with glee.

Boris and the Emperor, of course,
weren't having such a good day.

But at least one thing turned out well for the Emperor.
People *did* talk about him for years to come...

The Gingerbread Man

Once upon a time, many years ago,

a little old woman

108

and a little old man
    lived on a farm.

109

They were kind people.

It made them sad that they had no children.

"If only we had a little boy," sighed the old woman.

"I know!" she said one day.
"I could make a boy out
of gingerbread!"

So she took out her recipe book.
She weighed and she measured,

she mixed and
she stirred,

she rolled the dough
and she cut out a shape.

Then she put it in the oven to bake.

Soon the kitchen was filled with the smell of hot gingerbread.

"Almost ready now," said the old woman,
and opened the oven to look.

Mmmm

Out jumped a little gingerbread man!

He pattered across
the kitchen floor...

...and ran right out
of the open door!

"Stop!" called the old woman.

"Stop, stop!" called the old man.

But the gingerbread man
ran along the road, singing:

Run, run, as fast as you can,
You can't catch me
I'm the gingerbread man!

He raced past a horse
and a cow, grazing in the meadow.

"Mmm, you look delicious,"
neighed the horse.

"Come here, little man," mooed the cow.

But the gingerbread man ran along the road, singing:

I have run away from a little old woman and a little old man,
and I can run away from you too, yes I can!

Run, run, as fast as you can,
You can't catch me
I'm the gingerbread man!

He sped past a farmer,
hard at work in a field.

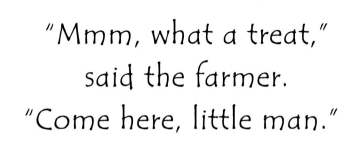

"Mmm, what a treat,"
said the farmer.
"Come here, little man."

But the gingerbread man ran along the road, singing:

I have run away from a horse, a cow,
a little old woman and a little old man,
and I can run away from you too, yes I can!

Run, run, as fast as you can,

You can't catch me
I'm the gingerbread man!

He scampered past a school,

and all the children shouted,
"Mmm, we love gingerbread!
Come here, little man!"

But the gingerbread man ran along the road, singing:

I have run away from a farmer in a field, a horse, a cow,
a little old woman and a little old man,
and I can run away from you too, yes I can!

Run, run, as fast as you can,

You can't catch me

I'm the gingerbread man!

On and on he ran,
until he came to a river.

He wanted to cross it, but
he was afraid of getting wet.

A fox spotted him.
"If you climb onto my
tail, I'll help you across,"
he said.

The fox started swimming with the gingerbread man on his tail.

Soon, though, his tail was dragging in the water.

"I'm so sorry," said the fox.
"Do climb onto my back."

But soon the water was lapping over the fox's back.

"I'm so sorry," said the fox.
"Do climb onto my head."

The gingerbread man tiptoed
up to the fox's head...

128

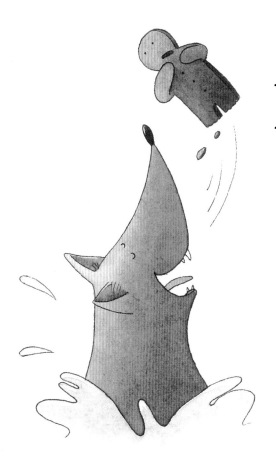

The fox tossed his head, and SNAP!
The gingerbread man was a quarter gone.

SNAP! He was half gone.

SNAP! Three quarters gone...

SNAP! And that was the end of him.

Quack! Quack!

The Story of Pinocchio was written by Carlo
Collodi, an Italian writer and a schools' advisor.
His real name was Carlo Lorenzini, but he used Collodi
as his writing name, after the village
of Collodi where he was born.

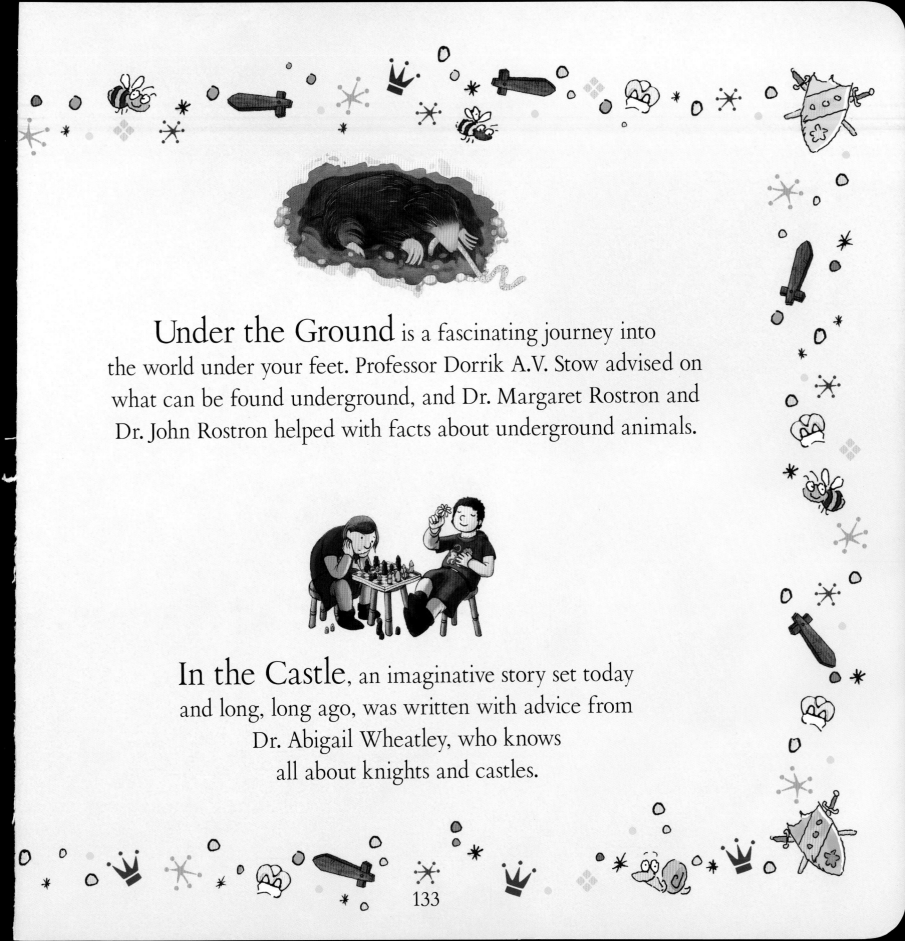

Under the Ground is a fascinating journey into the world under your feet. Professor Dorrik A.V. Stow advised on what can be found underground, and Dr. Margaret Rostron and Dr. John Rostron helped with facts about underground animals.

In the Castle, an imaginative story set today and long, long ago, was written with advice from Dr. Abigail Wheatley, who knows all about knights and castles.

The Emperor's New Clothes was first told by Hans
Christian Andersen, who was born in Denmark in 1805.
He was the son of a poor shoemaker but grew up
to write hundreds of fairy tales.

The Gingerbread Man is a story that has been around for centuries and it is known, in one form or another, all over Europe and America.

Designed by Andrea Slane, Louise Flutter,
Laura Parker and Katarina Dragoslavic.
Cover design by Katrina Fearn
Edited by Jenny Tyler, Lesley Sims and Gillian Doherty.
Additional design by Helen Edmonds and Caroline Spatz.

First published in 2007 by Usborne Publishing Ltd, 83-85 Saffron Hill, London EC1N 8RT, England.
www.usborne.com Copyright © 2007 Usborne Publishing Ltd. The name Usborne and the devices ♀ ⊕ are Trade Marks
of Usborne Publishing Ltd. All rights reserved. No part of this publication may be reproduced, stored in a retrieval system,
or transmitted in any form or by any means, electronic, mechanical, photocopying, recording or otherwise,
without the prior permission of the publisher. First published in America in 2008. UE. Printed in China.